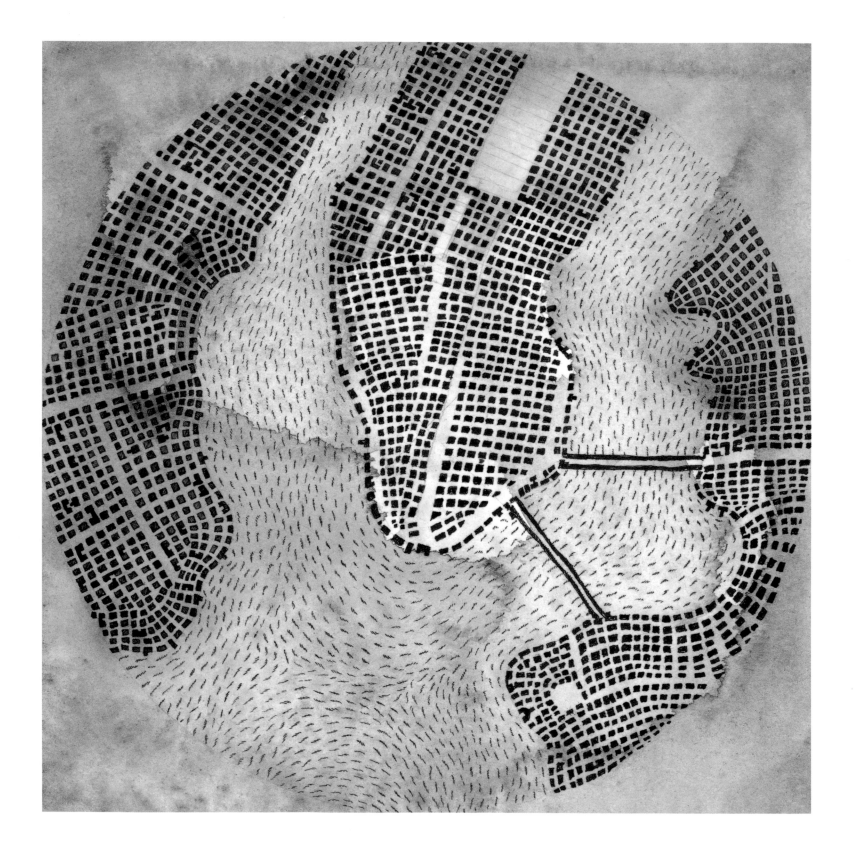

Peter Sís

MADLENKA'S DOG

Frances Foster Books

Farrar Straus Giroux · New York

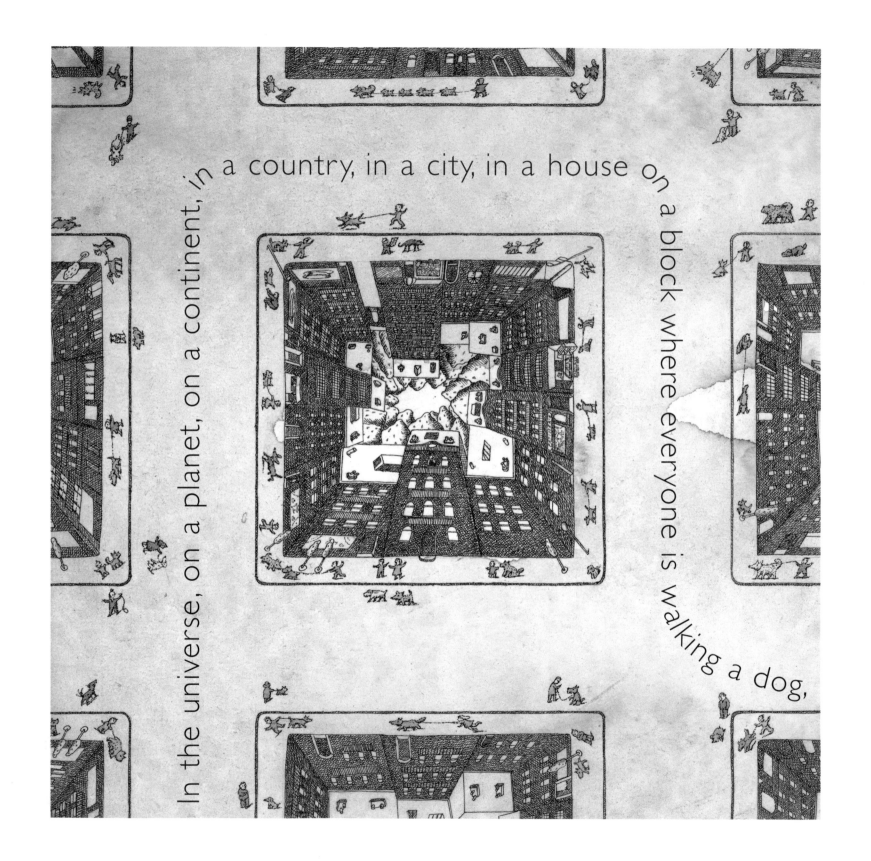

In the universe, on a planet, on a continent, in a country, in a city, in a house on a block where everyone is walking a dog,

there lives a girl named

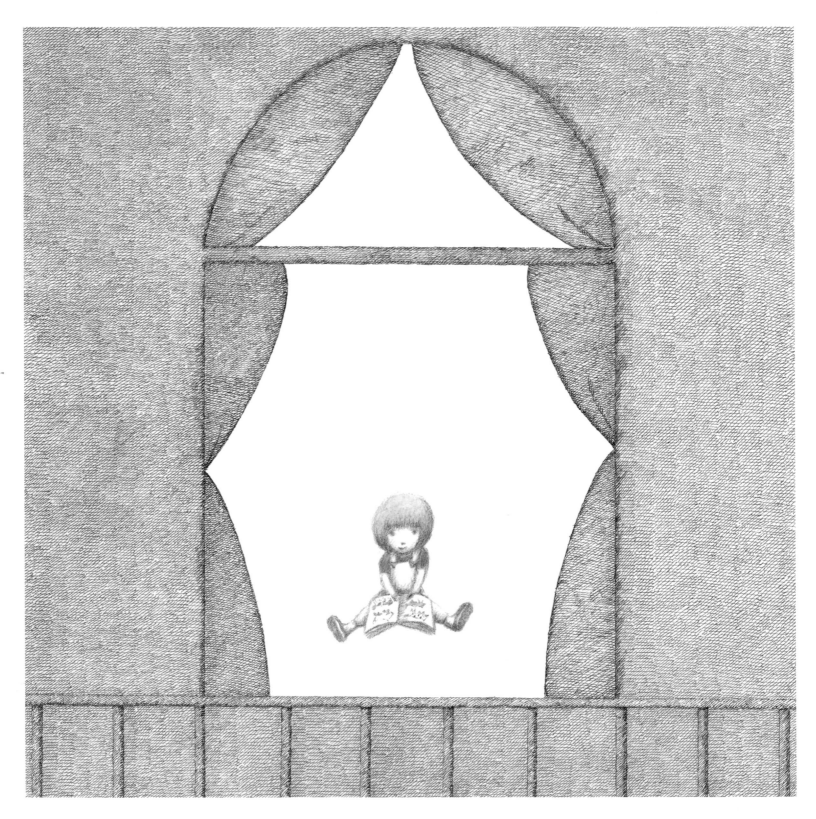

Madlenka

who wants a dog very much.

I want a dog!

Please, may I have a dog?

Oh! What's that?

Come here, little one.

Let's go for a walk.

Don't pull, little doggie.

Let's go around the block.

Madlenka and her dog meet Mr. Gaston, the baker.

Hello, Mr. Gaston. I have a new dog!

Bonjour, Madeleine. I once had a dog. Hello, dog.

Look, everyone. I'm walking my dog.
Oh, he's white and short, says Mr. McGregor.

No, he's big and woolly, says Mr. Eduardo.
Well, I like his spots, says the tourist.

Hey, everybody. Do you like my dog?

Yes! Ja! Hai!

Hi, Cleopatra. I have a dog!

e! Let's play in the courtyard.

Hi, Madlenka. I have a horse! Let's play in the courtyard.

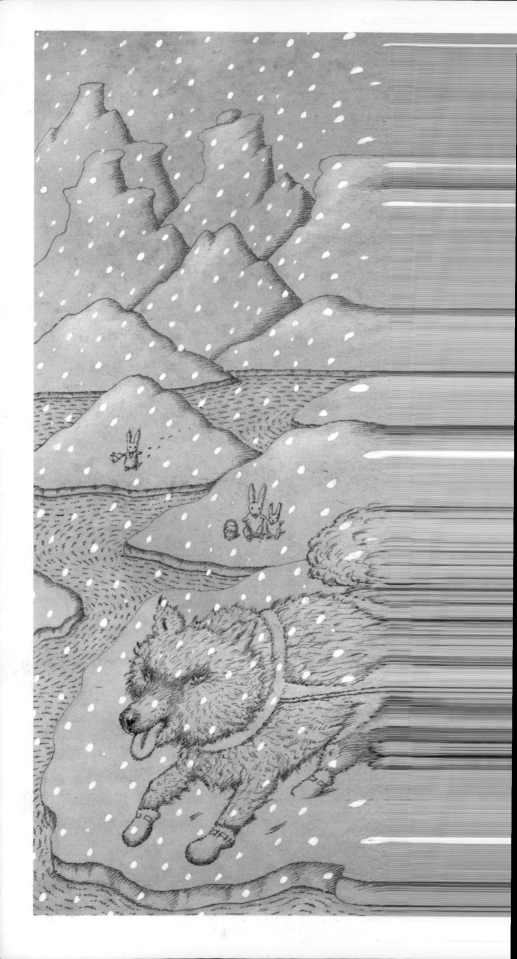

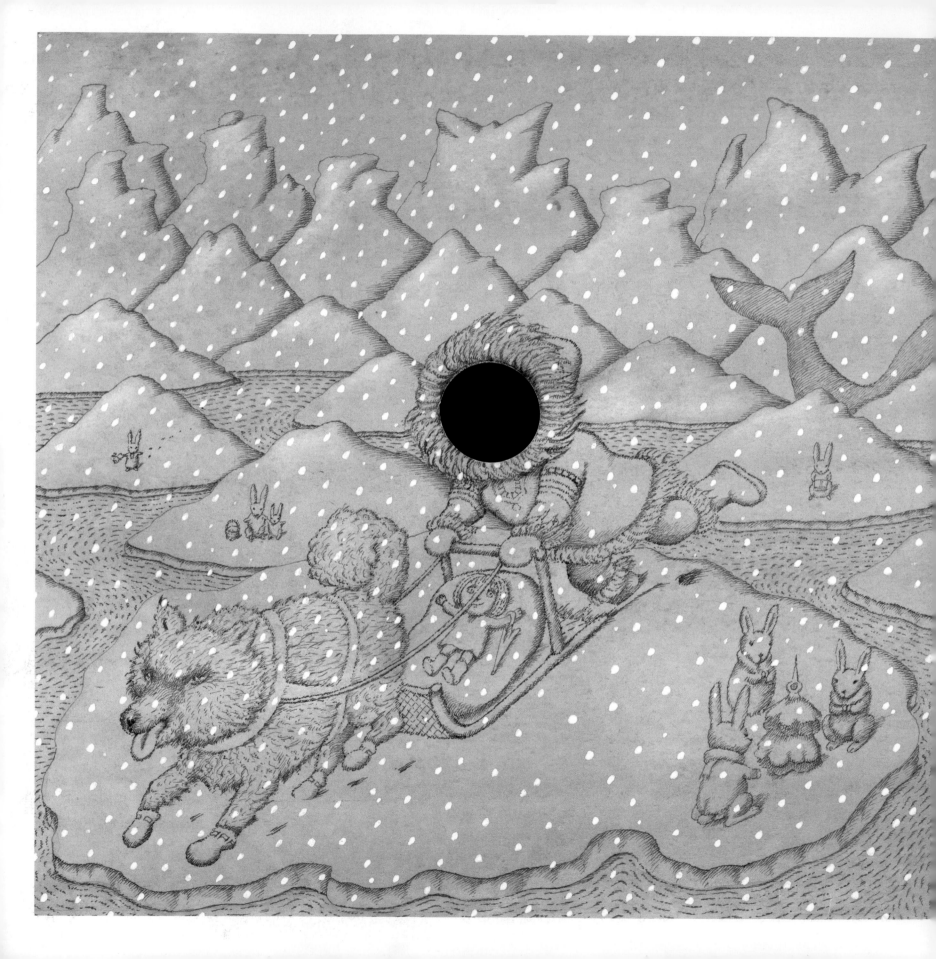

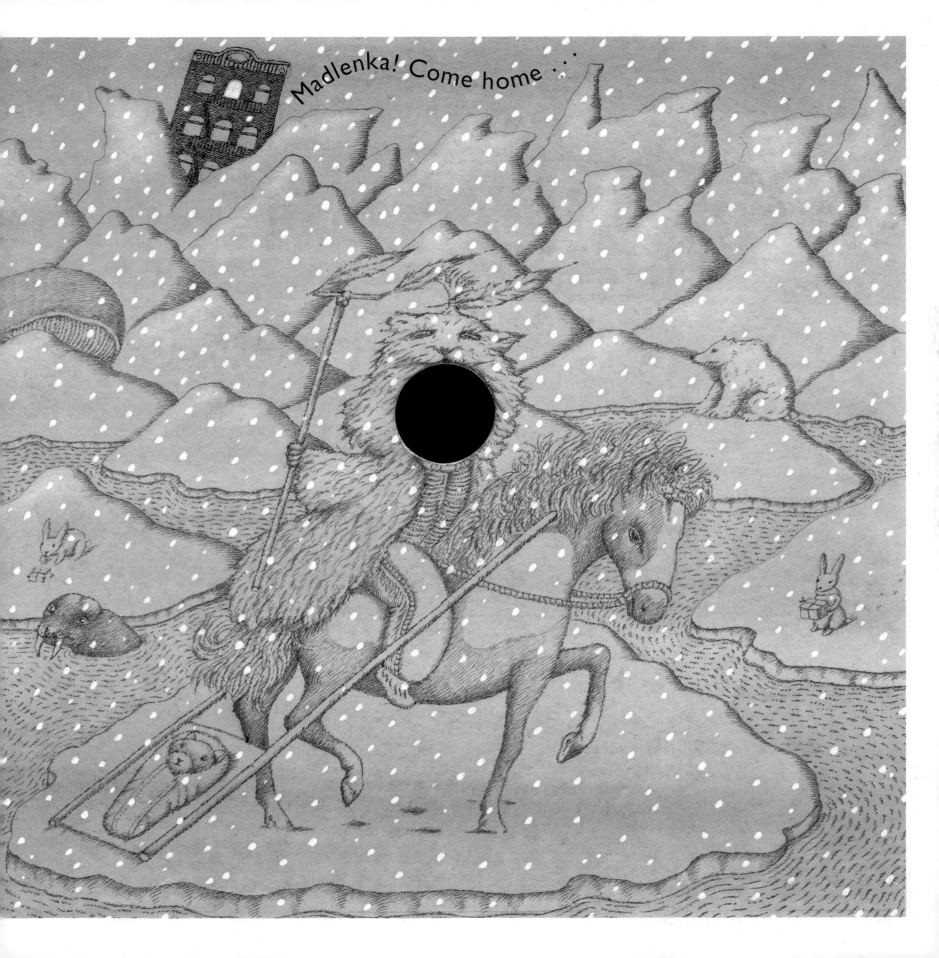

Bye-bye.

See you later.

Let's go, little doggie.

I'm home!

St. Bernard	Dalmatian	Maltese	Labrador Retriever	Scottish Terrier	German Shepherd	Basset Hound
Poodle	Pekingese				Boston Terrier	Yorkshire Terrier
Greyhound	Newfoundland				Old English Sheepdog	Husky
Bloodhound	Schnauzer				Cocker Spaniel	Dachshund
Golden Retriever	Boxer				Afghan Hound	Bedlington Terrier
Doberman Pinscher	Spitz				Bull Terrier	West Highland White Terrier
Pug	Foxhound	Great Dane	Cairn Terrier	Bulldog	Kerry Blue Terrier	Collie

● **Madlenka**

○ **Cleopatra**, Madlenka's school friend

● **Mr. Gaston**, the baker

● **Mr. McGregor**, the firefighter, member of FDNY Pipes and Drums

● **Eduardo**, the greengrocer

● **Vladimir**, the tourist

● **Mr. Mingus**, the musician

● **Ms. Grimm**, the former opera diva

● **Michiko**, the artist

Little doggie, Madlenka's invisible dog